SOON AND WHOLLY

- WESLEYAN POETRY -

Also by Idra Novey

SOON AND WHOLLY
IDRA NOVEY

with images from Erica Baum

WESLEYAN UNIVERSITY PRESS
Middletown, Connecticut

WESLEYAN UNIVERSITY PRESS

Middletown CT 06459

www.wesleyan.edu/wespress

Designed and composed in Albertina by Eric M. Brooks

Manufactured in the United States of America

Library of Congress Cataloging-in-Publication Data

NAMES: Novey, Idra, author. | Baum, Erica, illustrator.

TITLE: Soon and wholly / Idra Novey ; with images from Erica Baum.

DESCRIPTION: First edition. | Middletown, Connecticut : Wesleyan University
Press, 2024. | SERIES: Wesleyan poetry | SUMMARY: "Poems wrestling
with the pursuit of a meaningful life, both rural and urban, on a swiftly
heating earth" — Provided by publisher.

IDENTIFIERS: LCCN 2024008402 (print) | LCCN 2024008403 (ebook) |
ISBN 9780819501288 (cloth) | ISBN 9780819501295 (ebook)

SUBJECTS: LCGFT: Poetry.

CLASSIFICATION: LCC PS3614.O928 S66 2024 (print) |
LCC PS3614.O928 (ebook) | DDC 811/.6 — dc23/eng/20240223

LC record available at https://lccn.loc.gov/2024008402

LC ebook record available at https://lccn.loc.gov/2024008403

5 4 3 2 1

For my father
and for my sister Becca

What is not grasped has all
the chances of becoming real.

- EDMUND JABÈS,
  translated by Rosemarie Waldrop

CONTENTS

NEARLY

When we slid out of the lane.

When my sleeve caught fire.

While we fought in the snow.

While the oncologist spoke.

As the oil spilled.

While your retina bled.

While the woman at the shelter.

Beyond the gate to the forest.

While the forest turned to ashes.

While I escorted my father out.

After I led my brother in.

When your hand closed over mine.

When the dolphin reached the derelict canal.

While the cameras filmed it dying.

While the blackout continued.

When the plane dipped.

When the bank closed.

While the water.

While the water.

And we drank it.

STILL LIFE WITH INVISIBLE CANOE

Levinas asked if we have the right to be, the way I ask my sons if they can be trees.

The way the word tree makes them a little animal, dancing up and down like bears in movies.

Bears, I have to say, pretend we're children.

At a river, one of them says.

So we sip it, pivot in the hallway, call it a canoe.

It is noon and noon.

We are rowing in a blue that is a feeling mostly.

The way canoeing in the green under real trees is a feeling near holy.

O EARTH: AN ESTRANGEMENT IN SIX PARTS

12:05 p.m.

July, and I sit crisping inside a high-rise.

Cross-legged on the couch, I snack on data.

My days remain the temperature I assign to them while others go on sweating with no lucky dial on the wall.

The whale of this imparity swallows me, leaves me all mouth.

Inside the whale, I go on sipping my conditioned air.

2:36 p.m.

Two children wake and say they're mine.

Like a thief, I try to pocket my apocalypse scenes.

The children want the world, and I assure them they can have it.

I just have to find my sunglasses, can't see the planet anymore without them.

Except someone has sat on my only pair, and the children say it was me.

Entirely possible, I tell them, wishing irony could solve things.

Naked-eyed, I bowl into the brightness.

3:14 p.m.

We reach the closest public green, our place to mock-race over fake grass.

I urge the children to run as far as the hem of fences will allow.

In a stream once, when one of the children was me, I pressed on a mound of wet leaves.

My foot sank into a softness, the rotting chest wall of a dead deer underneath.

Until my ankle was trapped in those ribs, I hadn't considered how the unknowable might get hold of me.

In the plastic grass of our city, I track the back and forth of my offspring, feel my skin burning beneath the promise, our cream.

4:03 p.m.

I find a tree with some inches of shade, cower beneath it, consider how much of the lonely I came to know as a child in that wooded place was meanness.

The classmate spitting tobacco into his library book, the one setting fire to the gas-soaked nest of a bird, didn't they add us all up to less?

We drove past the forest more than we entered it, hoping against a sudden animal at the curve.

People crashed often into animals, and staying alive was knowing it—how fast a deer may dart when startled, appear at the bend of any road.

7:10 p.m.

I surrender to the cool of our rented walls, declare the sun irrelevant, pull every curtain down against it.

I let the tub water run till it warms, begin my nightly aligning of inanimate eyes.

The sacred adjustments come next, the fluffing of plush bears, of a stuffed octopus-shaped pillow — its limp tangle of tentacles.

I find my son's missing goat and Paddington, without which he doesn't know how to tip his mind into sleep.

7:41 p.m.

Before approaching the compost bin, I suck in some Twitter, sip a few more minutes of conditioned air.

Then I descend and re-enter the heat, deliver myself to the sightless, writhing gods of the bin.

I imagine their mouths multiplying inside me, gnawing an acropolis of my softer parts.

My hands release the sandy raisins I came to offer, the melon rinds I saved for them, after which I ascend, lighter.

Floor by floor, I rise again to my chosen temperature, picture the bin gods still chewing through me, a few of my particles redeemed.

VALUE CITY

Under the marked-down dresses, we conjured trips to Oslo.
Also to Lima. Mel says the game was my idea, hiding
behind hundreds of hems, inventing trips to cities we knew

only as pleasing arrangements of letters, places we'd likely
never see. Mel says it's how she remembers me: cross-legged, knotting
lengths of licorice, traveling the planet under racks of final sales.

A rhinestone belt fell on my head once, she says, and I kept on talking
about Alaska, the claws of king crabs we'd crack open and taste
the arctic, find out what we were missing at Red Lobster. Our travels

to nowhere, she says, lasted beyond the training bras
we compared in the dressing room. So what explains it, my failure
to recall these conjured trips, or why my psyche delivers words

from a woman I never sat with under packed rows
of dresses—the poet Fanny Howe asking what keeps the temple
of imagination *burning with candles against all odds,* whether it remains

behind a nipple and a bone? This fraught asymmetry with Mel occurs
after our nipples became a milk source. We're older, bowling by chance
in adjacent lanes, recognizing each other mostly from the bodies

of our children—echoes of ourselves in their noses, a familiar drop
in their shoulders. How's it possible, Mel asks, you recall none of it,
not even the red stickers that stuck to our palms? You must

remember picking off those stickers, she insists — amid news
of her divorce, her interest in crystals. I deliver trivia
about my long-haired sons bowling into the gutter, about my brother

who bowls much better and still lives in town. New pins lower
like sets of dentures, get swept again into the open jaws
of our separate lanes. There's no saying it: my betrayal. How else

to name the absence of our game in my mind? The thick clouds
over Lima, I remember; I got there after college, saw
the bronze rear of Pizarro's horse before protesters heaved

his pedestal to the ground. Alaska too I got to see, confused
the sound of calving glaciers with the blasts of rifles
I knew here, where Mel's continued through forty years

of deer season, the few weeks each November
for shooting bears. If I'd stayed, had Oslo remained
a sonic cluster, would my lack of recall rub less? Guilt

is what floods me at my swift retrieval of Fanny Howe's lines
but not the hems in Value City. I tell Mel the rhinestone belt
must've done something to my brain. We hug, exchange numbers

we'll never use. If there's a temple beyond glands and bone
for all that goes blank in a lifetime, maybe it resides in the body
of a poem, in meanings left between the spread knees

of enjambment. The next bowlers go live on the lane screens:
Eddie Wins, JP the Dream Pony, La Reina Carla, CU
on the Moon. Reader, some of these names are flourishes

for the sake of this poem. Eddie Wins, he's up there. Also Carla,
but with no bravado. CU on the Moon is true; someone assuming
our lane has lunar plans and wants a companion. Maybe Carla.

Maybe JP, who prefers to keep his dream pony to himself.

THE DUCK SHIT AT CLARION CREEK

We liked to stick it in a BB gun and shoot it.

We tattooed with it.

We said Hallelujah, the poor man's tanning lotion.

Then the frack wells began, something black capping the water and we got high watching a green-backed heron die.

We got funny at Clarion, flung each other's underwear into the trees.

Why was it we got naked there like nowhere else?

Maybe we knew we were getting rusted inside as the trucks we rode into the water.

Maybe we only appeared to be floating, but soon and wholly we'd go under, get sucked to the bottom.

We'd sink and become creek bed; its deep mud would claim us, hold us hard and close.

THE RESIDENT *LEOPARDUS JACOBITA*

Customers ask in the bookstore about the cat's abundance of silvery fur, its paws large as a dog's.

The bookstore staff assure them the cat is calm and do not mention their hope that it will vanquish the rats around the back dumpster, and indeed within a week the rats are gone.

Soon, people come in just to experience the cat's feral stare, to comment on the thickness of its silvery tail.

A bookseller posts a T. S. Eliot quote about cats withholding a secret, ineffable name.

At Sunday story time, the cat lunges at a baby in a gray-eared hat and the question of banishment begins.

A bookseller skims a cat encyclopedia, finds an entry for *Leopardus jacobita*: a silvery wild feline that hunts high in the Andes.

The similarity is uncanny, and the chinchilla, its prey of choice, has the same grayish ears as the infant hat.

Visitors begin to stare at the cat longer from further away, murmuring like witnesses around a deathbed.

By spring, the *Leopardus jacobita* weakens.

It no longer catches rats, hardly leaves the couch at all.

One Tuesday, they find it motionless, a passing as quiet as any creature in a bookstore, sensing it may be the last of its kind.

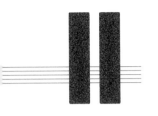

THAT'S HOW FAR I'D DRIVE FOR IT

for the poet H.G., who never published her poems

I'm in the car with Helen, supreme guide to proceeding otherwise.

My relatives refused to travel hours for a rhubarb, but Helen said: Why get out of bed, if not for a private quest of minor significance to anyone else?

It's a question of libido, she said, sometimes you wake up craving sex.

Other days a hunger comes for shoveling, to dig up whatever your relatives deem worthless.

All it takes to stymie a private quest is one fallen tree over the road.

To proceed, we had to turn back—resign ourselves to the snaking nature of progress.

Once more we drove through Tyrone, a township of farms and tire stores, a garage in which a boy burned his eyebrows off tinkering with wires under a car and became my grandfather.

I was named for someone before him who didn't begin her life here, never learned to write in English, yet still managed to plant something that perennially thickened, red and edible.

Beneath us, the cement ended on a road with no name.

Over rutted gravel, we discussed what was compelling us to continue — if it was libidinal, or if it was something simpler, mere stubbornness.

We didn't bother talking about being lost; we had no hunger for stating the obvious.

Helen said maybe a fellow human would appear if we played better music.

We belted Tina Turner and it worked: we found humanity — a woman exiting a house, a man behind her with a strip of white hair like a skunk tail.

These are the people, Helen said. They will know what we need to know.

In ten minutes, they delivered us.

We reached the yard where my namesake's rhubarb had returned, unbidden, for a century.

My father scoffed at so much gas and distance for a plant I could buy at any garden store.

My stepmother predicted futility, said whatever I did or not, the rhubarb would die on the hot long ride to the home I've chosen elsewhere.

But the real question, Helen said, is how your family lived these hours instead.

Are they dancing right now, are they singing Nutbush City Limits with Ike and Tina? Are they making out, even considering taking off their clothes?

Trisha Brown said: Dance is a disruption of the everyday.

See also: the ineffable; what stirred Helen to join me, to refine her gorgeous poems and pile them in a drawer.

A year later, she nearly died.

Recalling her near-death, Helen spoke of our trip, bringing our bodies all those miles to a stranger's yard.

To break up the ground around the root clumps we'd come for, the current owner jumped onto the step of his shovel.

He gave me a shovel to use my weight and jump as well — a duo disruption of the everyday.

We circled and loosened the earth, spoke only in gestures.

It was a dance as transcendent as anything I've purchased tickets to attend.

Helen almost died at four a.m. on a solo drive to a flea market.

She forgot to click her seatbelt, had taken a sleeping pill that caused a blackout in the car.

Yet the blackout didn't end her.

A lack of audience for her poems didn't either.

My namesake's rhubarb didn't perish on its hot travel over various states to new ground.

Its leaves have grown broad as the ears of elephants, as the living elements of ancestral presence I'd been craving.

My son churned the ruddiest stalks into sorbet.

He chopped up its petioles with strawberries into pies.

Meaning is a hunger. Some of us need to eat and eat it.

I've got a bridge to show you, Helen told me after she didn't die.

The most magnificent bridge collapse into a muddy river you've ever seen, she said.

To really sate the libido for symbolic experience, she told me, we could strip and swim right under it.

TOO SOON TO TELL

- with images from Erica Baum -

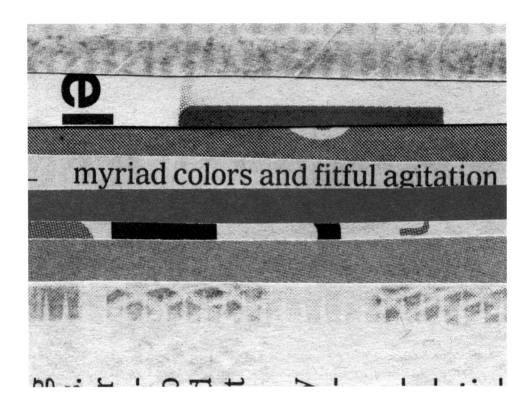

myriad colors and fitful agitation

March

How long can you remain smooth and reflective as a full glass of water?

Or will your stillness be more like vinyl, some kind of matter through which sound can pass but no luck with light.

Are you growing dim, is the question.

Has the heat index started to melt your senses.

Why does it feel like a sign of life to misbehave with punctuation, end a question with a period.

To answer yes to someone in the dark, even to yourself, has the faint sound of color.

In dimming days, you find one way to break the grip of stillness is blinking.

Exercising your iris sends a message to your mind: it is not yet made of vinyl.

Your eyes still have a calling; they strain for light.

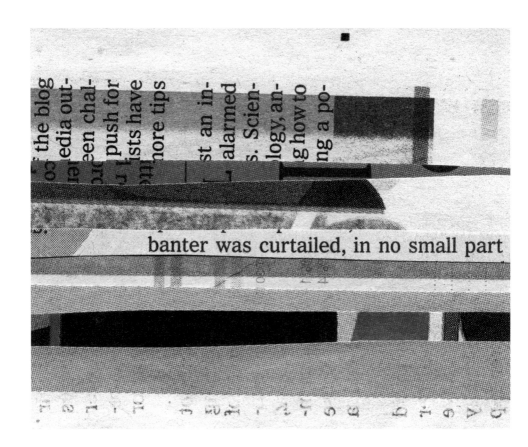

the blog
edia out-
en chal-
push for
sts have
ore tips

st an in-
alarmed
s. Scien-
logy, an-
g how to
ng a po-

banter was curtailed, in no small part

Early April

Perhaps now is the time to play guitar again with the kind of exuberance that came to you in high school.

Within the fixed lines of another mandated day inside, you sit before the caked dust on your guitar case.

You wipe a bit, lift the lid and peer in, recall sitting with this same instrument in the woods during high school, a few hours after rain.

Drops fell from the trees, dampened the velvet emptiness inside the case.

Other drops drummed thumb-like against your guitar's hollow body.

Beyond your apartment now, more sirens shatter the air.

Inside, you sit with your guitar, imagine rain playing it for you.

by putting you in her shoes, and   "A Monster

BY THANKSGIVING

Late April

Beyond your window, the calmest voices belong to people speaking to dogs.

These one-sided dialogues have become as entrancing to you as rain landing in the velvet hollow of your guitar case.

Maybe you are honing a skill during this long spill of days inside.

The skill of listening with your arms still, no device in your hands.

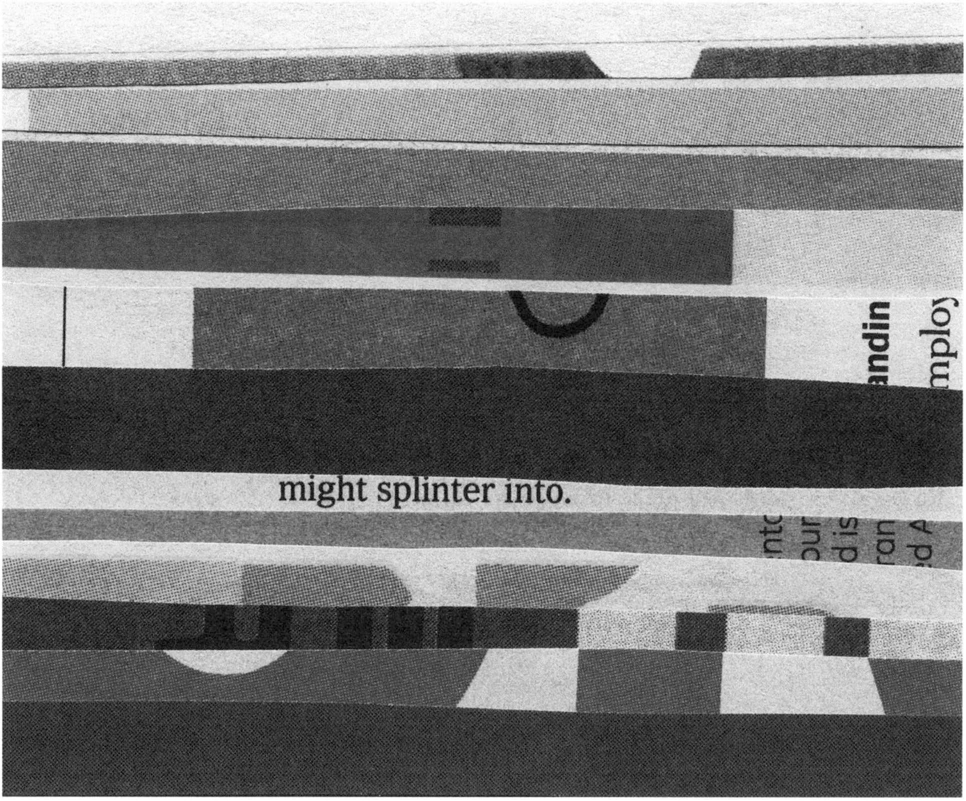
might splinter into.

May

Your theme for the evening is desolate breakfast.

With each week of the same spoon, the injustice of who keeps dying and who doesn't becomes more brutal and bewildering.

Your sister who is essential leaves her apartment each night for the hospital.

She tells you her nights are fractus—every hour another jagged fragment of cloud.

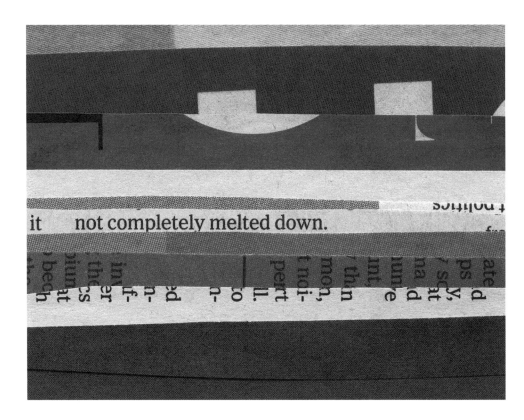

June

The light bulbs burn out all at once in your living room.

In the darkness, you remember you still have the alphabet and turn it on.

You tap at the keys and fear you're hitting every third letter wrong.

You go on tapping regardless.

Naming where you aren't, words come faster in the dark.

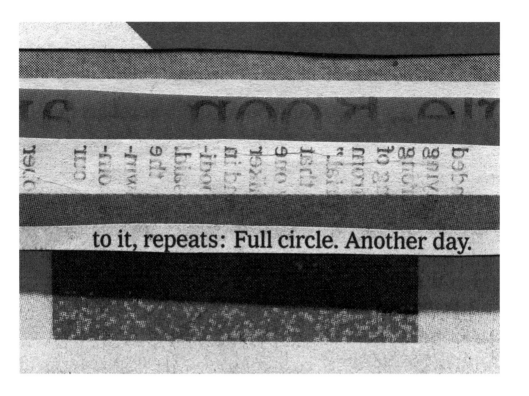

to it, repeats: Full circle. Another day.

July

You ask the plane tree outside your window about your motionlessness,
your role in the atrocities on monstrous repeat.

You memorize the long list of names someone's taped to the trunk and
don't need the tree to answer.

You stand and find your shoes.

BLUE SILO AND A BONFIRE

for Guillermo and Jodie

After two years in masks, we gathered at the Maciels' farm, chopped at weeds grown tall as our children — at burdock, with its thick burrs that dug into the skin.

We cut the nettles down, all the stinging weeds that stuck to us and to the sheep, lodged in the paws of the dogs.

The burrs pricked through our shoes and jeans, wounded our hands when we moved through the field, wanting to feel something wild within ourselves.

No matter where on the stem my son gripped the nettles, no matter what chopping tool he brought from the barn, the weeds got hold of him.

J's whole back turned into a map of burrs, his same back struck last year by a car, the back he bent now to feed the fire, bent with his long responsibility for his mother, and his despair at how fast she was going blind.

We all bent, attempted to get the burdock out of each other's hair as our heap blazed high enough to heat our faces if we drew closer.

And we drew that close, over and over — poking the flames with our sticks, with our half-built houses and mounting debts.

We poked the flames with our misspoken words and cancer scares, with our dread for the whole heating earth.

We leaned into the weedfire with all the wavering love we could stand receiving from each other.

With three flashlights between us, we slashed and yanked at whatever we could in the dark, knowing the burdock would seed and grow right back, release new burrs into the wooly sides of the sheep.

We knew whichever of us was not ill or gone was still getting along and not too caught up chopping at some other field, would be lucky to bend again here, cut down another day's worth of spiky burrs just to ignite them, watch their hot shapes enliven the blue metal of the silo.

To behold this fire of stinging weeds even once together left us brighter, to see the smoke of what stung rise in front of us, burn a path into the indifferent sky.

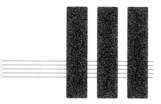

REGARDING MARMALADE, COGNATES, AND VISITORS

July

V arrives, expects nothing
but to witness our lives and find kindness
and why shouldn't she
but for the boiling water my partner spills
on my arm and the FUCK'S SAKE
that escapes my mouth now the snout
of the spitting mammal in me.
If there's a craft to the failing of simple
expectations, I've mastered it
and majestically — but if there's something
that must be said, it must be said,
Lispector says of a woman entering
an empty room and finding a version
of herself so dark it makes her pause
and really see it, how she's no better
than the cockroach in her closet
so she eats it.

August

O looks totaled,
older but more wholly
himself as we kiss in the tradition
of his country, where he kissed
a man recently and told
his wife, and things ended,
this man who bends now
to kiss my infant son
then we have nothing
to say—so good and startled
we are after altering
the particles of our lives,
until finally he asks
about my sadness
in his country, how it lasted
on and on and I tell him
it was the brown-yellow
of dead grass on a near hill,
then more distant, until the hill
was gone.

October

If our view were not a Holiday Inn
but a fringe of trees, I could say G-d here
is our greenly hidden.
                         If we lived
amid Joe Pye weed and high grass
instead of spackle and peeling plaster
I could say perhaps
                         I'm listening to G-d now
in the owl's hoot, a wind playing the silo,
a sticking sorrow,
                         any sound but the snore
of our latest visitor on the futon. Dear G-d,
please make him turn, make me kinder.
I'm not far from unfathoming it all.

November

To choose not to know:
the option.
        But there was

a small plastic device
that offered it,
        the whole knowing

in no more than a minute.
An instant
        translation of

what was beginning
in my body
        or wasn't.

I simply had to close
a door, bend
        over a device.

Dear S had arrived
to stand with me
        in the after

the two of us full as
clay pots with the dirt

        of knowledge.

December

F texts through breakfast, texts
through dinner, texts stepping in
and out of the bathroom, a towel
on his head. Texts as we talk
about literature and he zippers
his compact black valise, says Idra,
querida, never seen you
look better.

December, Still

The last bees have gone.
The quiet in my hive is

of wind licking a vacant house
and I am the vagrant inside, staking out

where to place my few thoughts
and boots. If I ought

to start a fire, let it undo
our rental living room.

January

Three days after A leaves, I see him still.
Naked in the kitchen, still gazing
at the holiday cards on the fridge.
I cower again, he covers his penis,
the winter season sleets on.

March

Something's gone and spilled
in our speakers, or why else
does M sound this altered—
her voice metallic and skittering,
static
        then fumbling out.

We get up from the couch,
sit back down, speak in Spanish
then English, wait for M
to hold another note, let it float
like pollen over an open street.

April

Does no dishes, dribbles sauce
across the floor. Is more dragon
than spaniel, more flammable
than fluid. Is the loosening
in the knit of me, the mixed-fruit
marmalade in the kitchen of me.
Wakes my disco and inner hibiscus,
the Hector in the ever-mess of my Troy.
All wet mattress to my analysis,
he's stayed the loudest and longest
of any houseguest, is calling now
as I write this, tiny B who brings the joy.

June

I serve J a plate she doesn't take,
offer her a softer chair. We were close
as cognates once, nearly holy
to one another — which comes down now
to coming down
to what?
          To having been cognates once.
Swappable as the *agua* my son says
for the sky in his tiny find-the-world books.
And we find it — the same blue.

LETTERS TO C

- with images from Erica Baum -

a wave would be hear
to enfold the note
spraying its fo
music. I gr
my thing
struck
in

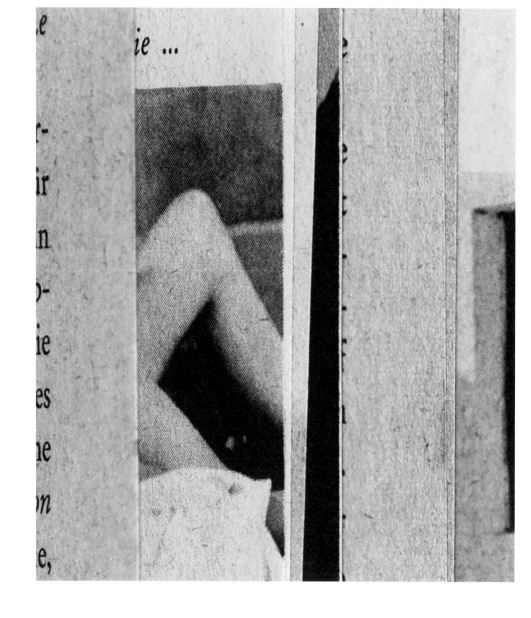

I

Dear C, I'm turning from.
Have been syntaxed and stirred into a purple.
Blurred to blind.
I made a mess of page twenty-two,
couldn't resurrect what you left unsaid
into words that wouldn't.
Do you believe in grieving?
I mean for language, the endangered
animal of, fleeing into caves.
I can only keep after it in fits
or I get trapped
in the keeping after. That,
and bliss.
Your spinning but devoted

I.N.

II

"The word that's missing in order to complete a
thought may take half a lifetime to appear."
- CLARICE TO FERNANDO, 1953

I've vanished
from waiting for the word that will.

The way my neighbor
backs up his car so fast he hits the trash bags

and they bury him.
And so is living for me, in the mis-appeared.

In the clear that will not,
Clarice. Your meanings lean like buildings

in the wind from.
You too worked as a translator, know one has to hang

the missing word
like a hat on a wall without a hook.

I'm either the hook
that could have or the hat which has to.

Falling now.

III

---

*"I know I'm using words that perhaps sound too
strong (I had a night of insomnia, believe me . . .)"*
- CLARICE TO FERNANDO, 1957

C, I dropped your sequence
in hot water. I talked
to the boil. I said Here
is my thumb for you to burn.
Here is the soft heart
of my hand and my arm
and the nape of my wreck.
I said vapor, just take me.
I'm done burning
with these pages. Being invisible
doesn't mean a person
won't blister, doesn't mean
the blisters won't fill
with pockets of water
or when lanced the rawest flesh
won't emerge. First the word
then the leak of water,
what another mind
may never skin.

IV

Down into
the night of it,
the blight of a word
from a dark farm
which may fog
continuously.

Down to
the symbol of it
and wondering
at five a.m. if
it's the winter
in translation
that makes people
distrust it, these dust-hours
of doubting.

Down again
to the hesitation
which may (or
may not) turn
into the stamen
of a flower—stamen loose
from the Greek
for man's house

and now
there's that lodge.

Down then
to etymology.
Or back to filament.
To flowering.
Up all night.

V

Dear author ghost,
dear desk, I've left you
for a man. The body
has its callings
after all.

Your mortal
but abiding

I.N.

VI

*"I'm working badly and badly on a romance or
novel, struggling against a very true impression
of futility."*
- CLARICE TO FERNANDO, 1954

Dear C,
feeling stuck today,
luckless, the puckered skin
around a scar.

At a luncheon,
a man tucked up to say
translation was once
considered women's work, did
I know it, lowly
as literary dishwashing.

Alchemy, too, I told him,
was seen once
as mere cooking —
with gold.

It grows so old,
the effort of diplomacy.
Did you ever
imagine vanishing
behind a giant
paper fan?

I picture the fan
covered with hundreds
of flying oven mitts
and cast-iron pans.

All soaring — airborne
as women
after centuries deferred.

VII

*". . . in a small daily life, in which a person risks
herself more deeply, with greater threats."*
- CLARICE TO FERNANDO, 1953

If a woman translates a woman who writes a woman who sculpts a
pleasant something out of small clutches of bread.

If the clatter of earrings.

If the clutches become less pleasant, can no longer be called the tender
rendering of bread.

If a woman translates a woman writes a woman who is less and less.

If the flesh of bread.

If folded between fingers.

If the word for deadline and rolling and oratorio.

If collapsing under.

If the matter with the clatter of earrings is.

VIII

C, I can't recall
who I was before the haunting handiwork
of translating you.

When the man at the store said, Miss,
you are dripping with it,
I thought he meant your novel.

And the unanswerables.
The false sanity of fancy language.

What was I failing at
before this — and why is it
failure makes a person feel
so irremediably alive?

This blue work.
This gluing of impossibilities.

Olhando ainda. Still looking.
Looking, still.

IX

"this is a letter for sharing news and complaints."

- CLARICE TO FERNANDO, 1953

These letters, C,
are my geese to you.
They come backward
in the formation of a letter
from an alphabet
that can only be flown.

So much geese-work
leaves me fat and baffled,
my vocabulary slack
with Latinates.

I miss my sleek years, slender
with the certainty of what I knew.
What's terrifying about you, C,
is that you know
what you don't know, what
none of us do.

But I have to go — my sons
want me to speak in puppet.
And so it is performing your words:
I'm a blue-faced creature
with seams between her fingers.
A being with no eyelids
who cannot blink.

X

". . . it's so hard to leave the routine of this house."

- CLARICE TO FERNANDO, 1957

I know all the frozen fish involved
in leaving a house and the fossils,
the upholstered impossibles.

For your green noon, C,

I tried to play the ballad
as you had it, crisply enough
to cut the strings of the balloon

and then cut the sky

into which lost balloons
become fugitives.

Your choosing green

for midday seemed
deeply blue to me. I heard
the unsaid color in it,

the thrum of moving darkly

along the brightness
of a house, the high of a word
in that silence.

I.N.

XI

"nearly eight months since Paulinho was born . . .
I drink fewer milkshakes and carry on a vacant,
agitated daily life."

\- CLARICE TO FERNANDO, 1953

A fantasy:
We are standing by a sandbox,
both lost
in the camouflage of those hours
and their boxes.
I ask about the pronoun you often place
before God
and you go on smoking.
The sun now
above the playground begins to burn
and then
the snow burns. My sons are grown.
At last
you turn to answer and I
am listening.

there will be now in my mouth.
not to finish ended. I am
the point? there one
long as I knew
know wise
it and

THE EXTRA PASSENGER

We were high in the Andes, seeking the hot springs we swam in ten years before.

Only now a mining company had moved things around.

We'd heard they slashed a glacier in half, diverted the flow of more rivers than they'd admitted.

We trusted a trickle of steaming water must still be bubbling up somewhere.

When a tire popped, we didn't take it as an omen to go back.

We installed a spare and drove higher, convinced the finding of a sulfur pool was just a matter of will.

The children asked how much longer, and why had we driven this far with so few snacks?

After one dizzying curve, a kid hunched over and purged enough liquid to circle his shoes.

Maybe the altitude was the cause; maybe the apocalypse—all the bleak zigzags of mining roads cutting through the stripped face of the cordillera.

Whatever had gone wrong inside this child's body, the clear liquid just kept coming, hot enough to steam.

His bile reached our sandals, tingled the undersides of our feet.

Is this the hot springs everyone keeps talking about, another child asked and who could blame her?

Born long after we last came here, she'd never experienced the goats, never got to kneel and see her face in those pools.

THE MAN WHO GAVE BIRTH TO A PANDA

He had to have it, his mother told him, how could he not? There were so few left in the world. He felt heaviest at night with the miracle inside him. He was a vessel now for the future of a species. What if he got up too fast and killed it?

Or maybe his stillness would do it, turn him into the man who failed to deliver one of the world's most endearing and endangered. And if—miraculously—the panda emerged alive and another appeared in its place, would he have to give his body over to that one as well, and another after that?

The man dreamed of the panda's tiny eyes opening inside him, the doctor's wide incision, a whirring pain, and then the furry thing emerging. Maybe the creature would take a shine to him, or that would be it—his bit part in the history of the future.

HOUSESITTING WITH APPROACHING FIRE

Dear friends,

The ash-fall is thickening here.
It's filming over your pool.

I tell the cats we'll be fine.
The flames won't reach us.
I remind them we're feline.
Occupied enough just pawing the ash from our teeth.

Although now the fire seems to be widening.
It's flaming closer, having its way with the neighbors' jacaranda.
Burnt petals keep alighting on your diving board.

Dear friends,

I know I should stop pretending to be another pet.
I should be hosing down your new roof instead.
Or grooming a mustache to join the firemen on the street.

But what can a poet in a borrowed house really offer in a spreading fire?
Maybe a few remarks on the art of denial.
Whether we learn it from our fathers.
Or from our mothers.
Until we learn it from everyone.

I've heard some fires do buckle on their own.
Knowing this could happen is consoling, makes it possible to curl up.
To go on dozing like a cat.

Dear friends,

I want to be lucky.
I'd very much like to go on licking my paws.

I want to seal more travel creams in ziploc.
I want to have it all.

YOUR REGARD, WORLD

after Ana Mendieta's Siluetas

The world said all we can see is your body and she said see it here, world, in an open tomb in Yagul, overtaken by flowers.

The world said women are most legible when committing acts of self-sabotage and she said demented, demeaning world, watch these rocks of yours, watch them heave and breathe as I emerge from beneath them.

She said watch me carve myself out of my own hands, she said here I am — coming out from under your endless dirt, world, making it give way to my knees and legs and if a sublime inversion of death from beneath your rocks isn't art, world, then what's your regard worth anyway?

She said watch this bright remaking into sand and the world said, outsider, we're not inclined to abide the sight of you with any kind of light.

The world said let's talk about your husband and she said please regard me from behind this mustache, this beard, this bleeding down my face.

She said world, you are green insect, specter, man to plant.

She said shadowy planet, a woman can catch the light despite you, can outlast, digitized in twigs, rocks, ash and gunpowder, can flame back a million times in burning silhouette.

MINOR KEY

After the newest continuous disaster, I move toward the windows and vex gently against the glass.

I vex once more against the impassive elevator door.

Some predict nothing less than a natural disaster trifecta could bring the northern hemisphere to collapse.

To hope harder, I buy overpriced hydroponic tomatoes, apologize longer to the wild lobster in the market.

We stare each other down through the gathering clouds in his tank.

ON RETURNING TO MY HOMETOWN IN 2035

Even the gun shows are gone now, even the scrapyards, the darkest, farthest barns.

The strip mall, half-empty since my elementary years, contains only chemicals now, the lot sequestered behind fences, its metal tanks checked each September for leaks in the seals.

I lost my virginity in a basement here, lost my balance on a backhoe, had to pick the gravel out of my knees.

For the prom, my date was the tank man just vanquished in the heat storm, his data screen open to augmented porn.

This morning in my Honda pedi-plane, I flew over where we used to sled, old hills oranged now for warning, only the edges still brown.

I saw a denier sitting outside in a lawn chair, her hair so long it met the ground.

There's no idling in the airways now, which is why I can't tell you if she was dying.

AFTERLIFE

She'd wanted forest.

She couldn't recall wanting to turn into a tree specifically, but those minutes in the hospital had been so loud, all the beeping machines and those agonizing sounds coming from her mother.

She remembered thinking *quiet*, the word *forest* surfacing and then something snapping inside her like a twig, a clean break—and she'd done it, delivered herself from that horrible, mechanized bed into the dense woods where she was born.

She was back in the mountains, turning more tree every second. Her back extending, her legs stiffening, and her head . . . what was happening to her head? Was it burl, wasn't that the name for those raised lumps on the bark that formed a network of buttons?

As a child, she'd loved running her fingers over those arboreal buttons, imagining if she pressed one just right, it might grant her entry into a tree's inner chamber.

Now she was a tree, with no feelings except in seeds and shadows.

ACKNOWLEDGMENTS

Some of these poems were previously published, in some cases in different versions.

"Nearly": *Poem-a-Day*, Academy of American Poets

"Still Life with Invisible Canoe": *Poem-a-Day*, Academy of American Poets

"O Earth: An Estrangement in Six Parts": *The Literary Review*

"The Duck Shit at Clarion Creek": *Poetry*

"The Resident *Leopardus jacobita*": Independent Bookstore Day Anthology, 2018

"That's How Far I'd Drive for It": *Poetry*

"Too Soon to Tell": Poetry Society of America's "In Their Own Words" series online, and in print as a collaboration with artist Erica Baum for Forma Gallery, UK (2022)

"Blue Silo and a Bonfire": *A Public Space* (published under another title)

"The Extra Passenger": an earlier, longer version appeared in *The Yale Review* and in the *Pushcart Prize Anthology 2023*

"The Man Who Gave Birth to a Panda": *Poetry Now* program/podcast on WNYC (New York Public Radio) and on the Poetry Foundation website

"Housesitting with Approaching Fire": *Guernica*

"Your Regard, World": *Hyperallergic*

"Minor Key": *Tin House*

"On Returning to My Hometown in 2035": *Poetry* and *Poetry International*

"The Afterlife" was featured in "4 Spooky Short Stories Inspired by Haunting Images" in *T, The New York Times Style Magazine* (October 31, 2018)

"Regarding Marmalade, Cognates, and Visitors" and "Dear C" were first published as a chapbook in the Cahier Series of Sylph Editions, in collaboration with series editors Daniel Medin and Dan Gunn. Individual poems from the chapbook were also published in *Poetry* and received a Contributor's Prize from that publication.

The quotation from Fanny Howe in "Value City" is from "A Hymn," in her book *Second Childhood* (Graywolf Press, 2019). The epigraphs for the series "Dear C" are my translations of quotations from Lispector in Fernando Sabino and Clarice Lispector's *Cartas Perto do Coração: Dois jovens escritores unidos ante o mistério da criação* (Editora Record, 2001).

My profound gratitude to Suzanna Tamminen, Jim Schley, and the magnificent team at Wesleyan University Press, to my agent PJ Mark, Michael Steger, and all at Janklow, to Erica Baum for our ongoing collaborations and for granting permission to include her artwork in this collection, to Nuar Alsadir, Jen Firestone, Helen Golubic, Garth Greenwell, Cathy Park Hong, Jenny Kronovet, Joseph O. Legaspi, Adriana Jacobs, Gerry Jonas, Katy Lederer, Alex Mar, Luis Muñoz, Greg Pardlo, Maggie Smith, Rene Steinke, and Monica Youn for their support, input, and the glow of their companionship, to Camille Dungy, Brigid Hughes, Dan Gunn, Daniel Medin, Meghan O'Rourke, Charif Shanahan, Tracy K. Smith, Erica Wright, Wendy Xu, and all the editors who selected iterations of these poems for publication, to the friends and relatives who contributed to the life of this book in myriad ways, to Leo, for his genuine interest in hearing every idea and poem for twenty-five years, and to Lázaro and Boaz who continue, every minute, to bring the joy. To my father and my sister Becca, who were alive until the last few poems, this book is for you.

LIST OF IMAGES BY ERICA BAUM

page 26
   "Fitful Agitation" (2020).
page 28
   "Banter Was Curtailed In No Small Part" (2020).
page 30
   "In Her Shoes" (2020).
page 31
   "Splinter" (2020).
page 32
   "Melted Down" (2020).
page 33
   "Full Circle" (2020).
page 49
   "Enfold" (2013).
page 50
   "i.e." (2012).
page 52
   "Interior New Chair" (2010).
page 55
   "Listen" (2013).
page 58
   "House" (2012).
page 62
   "Blonde" (2012).
page 65
   "Reflection" (2013).
page 69
   "The Point" (2013).

ABOUT THE AUTHOR AND ARTIST

IDRA NOVEY is the author of three novels, most recently of *Take What You Need*, a New York Times Notable Book of 2023 and finalist for the Joyce Carol Oates Prize. Her second poetry collection, *Exit, Civilian*, was chosen by Patricia Smith for the National Poetry Series. She is the co-translator with Ahmad Nadalizadeh of Iranian poet Garous Abdolmalekian's *Lean Against This Late Hour*, a finalist for the PEN America Poetry in Translation Prize in 2021. Her fiction and poetry have been translated into a dozen languages and she's written for the *New York Times*, *The Atlantic*, the *Washington Post*, and *The Guardian*. She teaches creative writing at Princeton University.

ERICA BAUM lives and works in New York City. She is known for her varied photographic series capturing text and images in found printed material, from paperback books to magazines, and from library indexes to sewing patterns. She received a BA in Anthropology from Barnard in 1984 and a MFA from Yale University School of Art in 1994. Her work is held in numerous collections, including the Whitney Museum of American Art, Solomon R. Guggenheim Museum, Metropolitan Museum of Art, Museum of Modern Art (MoMA, New York), San Francisco Museum of Modern Art (SFMOMA), and Musée d'art moderne et contemporain (MAMCO) in Geneva, Switzerland, among others.